MONSTER By Mistake!

Entertaining Orville

Adapted by **Mark Mayerson**

Edited by **Paul Kropp**

Based on the screenplay by
Mark Mayerson *and* **Kim Davidson**

Graphics by **Studio 345**

WINDING
STAIR
PRESS

Monster By Mistake
Theme Song

Hi my name is Warren and I'm just
a kid like you,

Or I was until I found evil
Gorgool's magic Jewel.

Then he tricked me and I read
a spell, now every
time I sneeze,

Monster By
Mistake…

My sister Tracy tries the
Spell Book. She
never gets it right.

But Tracy doesn't ever give
up, 'cause you know one day
she might

Find the words that will
return me to my former width
and height.

I'm a Monster By Mista….ah….ah…

I'm gonna tell you 'bout Johnny the
    Ghost,

He's a wisecracking,
    trumpet playing
    friend.

He lives up in the
attic (shhh…Mom and
    Dad don't know)

Johnny always has
    a helping hand
    to lend.

My secret Monster-iffic life always keeps
    me on the run.

And I have a funny
    feeling that the
    story's just begun.

Everybody thinks it's
    pretty awesome
    I've become

A Monster By Mistake!

I'm a Monster By Mistake!

I'm a Monster By Mistake!

Monster by Mistake
Text © 2002 by Winding Stair
Graphics © 2002 by Monster by Mistake Enterprises Ltd.
Monster By Mistake Created by Mark Mayerson
Produced by Cambium Entertainment Corp. and Catapult Productions
Series Executive Producers: Arnie Zipursky and Kim Davidson

National Library of Canada Cataloging in Publication Data

Kropp, Paul, 1948-
    Entertaining Orville

(Monster by mistake ; 3)
Based on an episode of the television program, Monster by mistake.
ISBN 1-55366-212-1

I. Moss, Cathy II. Cambium Film & Video Productions Ltd.
III. Title. IV. Title: Monster by mistake (Television program)
V. Series: Kropp, Paul, 1948– . Monster by mistake ; 3.

PS8571.R772E58 2002   jC813'.54   C2002-900356-3
PZ7.K93En 2002

Winding Stair Press
An imprint of Stewart House Publishing Inc.
290 North Queen Street, #210
Etobicoke, Ontario, M9C 5K4 Canada
1-866-574-6873

Executive Vice President and Publisher: Ken Proctor
Director of Publishing and Product Acquisition: Susan Jasper
Production Manager: Ruth Bradley-St-Cyr
Copy Editing: Martha Campbell
Text Design: Laura Brady
Cover Design: Darrin Laframboise

This book is available at special discounts for bulk purchases by
groups or organizations for sales promotions, premiums, fundraising
and educational purposes. For details, contact: Stewart House
Publishing Inc., Special Sales Department, 195 Allstate Parkway,
Markham, Ontario L3R 4T8. Toll free 1-866-474-3478.

1 2 3 4 5 6   07 06 05 04 03 02

Printed and bound in Champlain Graphics

COLLECT THEM ALL

8 BOOKS SO FAR!

Contents

Chapter 1

As soon as Warren read the magazine ad, he knew he had to have one.

"Tracy, come see this. It's so cool!"

"What are you talking about now?" Tracy asked her brother.

"This new computer game!" Warren said, pointing at the magazine ad. "Look at those graphics! Look at that display!"

Tracy was not impressed. The truth was, no computer game had ever impressed Tracy. She liked movies, books, her teen magazines and the odd video game . . . but that was it. Computers were only good for e-mailing her friends.

"Warren, calm down," she said. "Even if it's a great game, you don't have enough money."

Warren wasn't ready to give up. He zoomed down the stairs and came back with his Robbie the robot bank. Then he counted.

"I've got five . . . six . . . seven dollars. Maybe if you helped me?" He looked up at his sister with big eyes.

"I've got exactly eight dollars and twenty-six cents," Tracy replied.

Warren sighed. He did the quick mental math, but there was no way the total would even hit twenty bucks.

"Aw. We don't even have enough to buy the packaging."

Warren hit a couch pillow in frustration. The cloud of dust was almost enough to make him sneeze, but he held that back. Sneezing, you see, was a special problem for him. Ever since a mistake with a certain magic spell, Warren turned into a large blue monster each time he sneezed. Warren found this quite embarrassing. And they were both worried that their parents might find out.

"Hey, kid," Warren heard from over his head. Suddenly, the shape of Johnny the ghost became visible. "Sounds like you've got a problem."

"Hi, Johnny," Tracy said, greeting her friend. Johnny had been living up in their attic ever since his own house fell down.

"Hey, Tracy. I've got an idea for both of you, a smart way to make a little moolah."

"Moolah?" Warren asked.

"It's an old-fashioned word for cash," the ghost explained. "That computer game is probably over a hundred bucks. So why not set up an act and try to get yourself a few gigs."

"Gigs?" Warren asked. He was starting to feel pretty dense.

"Shows," Johnny explained. "Tracy knows a few magic tricks, so you two could put on a magic show. Hire yourself out for birthday parties. You could call it 'Tracy's Magnificent Magic Show.'"

"I like that," Tracy said.

"That's only because your name is in it," Warren told her.

"That's because I do the magic. I could use the jewel and the Book of Spells!" she said brightly.

Warren and Johnny both groaned. Tracy's record with using the Jewel of Fenrath and the Book of Spells was not a good one. She tried hard, but somehow she always managed to goof up the magic.

"Tracy," Johnny said, "maybe you should stick to some old-fashioned magic. You know, card tricks, disappearing rabbits, that kind of thing."

"Yeah," Warren agreed, "it would be safer. Besides I could be your assistant!" Now Warren was getting excited. Even if he were only Tracy's assistant, at least

they'd earn enough money to buy the game.

"Well, maybe," Tracy said. She went over to a trunk in the attic and pulled out an old top hat. "You could wear this."

Tracy quickly blew dust off the hat right into her brother's face.

"Ah . . . ah . . . ah-choo!"

Warren sneezed and immediately turned into the Monster, a seven-foot-tall blue giant.

"Oh, sorry, Warren," Tracy said. "I forgot."

The Monster just shook his very large head. There was no way the top hat would fit him now.

"But this gives me an idea," the Monster said. "I think I should be part of the show."

"Great idea, kid," Johnny agreed. "You get equal billing with your sister. 'Tracy's Magnificent Monster and Magic Show' – it'll be amazing."

Johnny was right, of course, but he couldn't have guessed how amazing the whole show would turn out to be.

Chapter 2

Warren and his sister didn't have to wait long for their very first job. The next day, they went out to put up posters. Tracy had done a fine job on the posters. The posters read:

**Tracy's
Magnificent Monster
and
Magic Show**

Warren was glad to get equal billing, but had some doubts about the Monster going public. They had worked hard to keep the Monster a secret. Only a few people in the town of Pickford had even seen the Monster. If people found out that Warren Patterson was really the

Pickford monster . . . well, they'd both be in big trouble.

Still, Tracy was determined. She figured that nobody believed in magic shows any more. But add a monster, and customers would be lining up around the block. All her brother had to do was sneeze.

"Warren," Tracy said. "How do you like this flower?"

"Flower!" Warren shouted. "That's ragweed. You know I'm

allergic to ragweed! It makes me . . . ah . . . ah . . . ah-choo!"

Warren finished his sentence by turning into the Monster.

"Did you have to do that?" the Monster snapped at Tracy.

"It's marketing," Tracy told him. "As Warren, you're pretty dull; but as the Monster you'll get us a job in no time."

Tracy was absolutely right. Just down the street, reading one of their posters, was a very well-dressed woman. She had a thin face and wore small glasses like a banker or a professor.

"Oh, child, are you the person who put up the poster?" the woman asked Tracy.

"Yes," Tracy said brightly. "I do the magic part of the show. And this guy," she pulled Warren around the fence, "this guy is the Monster!"

"Hmm, yes. Very good," she said,

inspecting Warren carefully. "Very good indeed."

"Thank you," Warren replied, disguising his voice. He winced as the woman pulled on his blue skin. She thought it was just a costume. Warren knew it was attached!

"I'd like to take advantage of your services," the woman said. "I'm looking for some entertainment for my son, Orville. My name is Mrs. Stein. The address is here on the card. I'd

like you to come by the house tomorrow at two. Two o'clock exactly."

"There is a small charge for our show, Mrs. Stein," Tracy said. "I'm afraid we don't take major credit cards."

"Cash won't be any problem, dear," replied the woman. "Your problem will be my son. You see, your job is to entertain Orville. And nothing – *nothing* – entertains Orville."

Chapter 3

The idea of doing a show seemed easy when Johnny the ghost first suggested it. But now that their first gig was coming up, Tracy and Warren were nervous. Tracy knew one or two magic tricks, but they hardly ever worked. And what would Warren do as the Monster? If he knew how to juggle or tap dance, that might be entertaining. But Warren didn't have those talents. In fact, Warren didn't have much talent at all.

Unfortunately, neither did Tracy.

"Don't get the jitters, kids," said Johnny the ghost. "I bet you'll bring down the house."

Warren moaned. "If Tracy uses the jewel and the Book of Spells, she just might."

"That's not what I mean. Bringing down the house means you're a big hit," Johnny told them. "Just keep up the patter, Tracy, and you'll amaze the kid with your tricks."

"I hope so," Tracy replied nervously.

Warren kept his mouth shut. The two of them had been rehearsing for hours. Tracy tried card tricks, disappearing tricks, all sorts of tricks. But she couldn't get them to work right. She'd even tried one with a rabbit that disappeared into a box. It took them an hour to get the poor rabbit unstuck.

It turned out that Tracy was no better with magic tricks than she was with real magic.

"Well, here we go," Tracy said as she and Warren walked up to the large house. Johnny the ghost disappeared as Mrs. Stein answered the door.

"Welcome, children. I'm so glad you're here on time. Now where is that monster? I believe he was part of the show."

"Oh, he's caught up in traffic," Tracy said. "But don't worry. He'll be here."

Mrs. Stein led Tracy and Warren into a very grand mansion. There were statues in the hall and paintings on the wall. In the background, the kids could hear a piano concerto by Beethoven.

"Pretty posh," Johnny the ghost said.

"What does that mean?" Warren whispered.

"Like classy, or rich," Tracy whispered.

Mrs. Stein didn't hear them; she was too busy lecturing. "Don't touch anything, children. These works of art are very precious."

"Oh, of course," Tracy said.

"Come this way, children," Mrs. Stein said. "I want to introduce you to my son, Orville." She took them down the hall, then shouted to her son. "Orville, Orville! The entertainers are here."

They found Orville sitting on the porch, playing with a plastic action figure. He turned out to be a quiet, neatly dressed boy with a very serious look on his face.

"Orville, what are you doing?" demanded Mrs. Stein.

"Oh, nothing," Orville replied, hiding the action figure.

"I hope all your work is done, young man. "Have you finished your French verb study?"

"Yes, Mother."

"Your math flash cards?"

"Yes, Mother."

"Your philosophy flash cards?"

"Yes, Mother. I did both Plato and Aristotle."

Tracy couldn't believe this. Little Orville was only six or seven, but he acted like an old man. He seemed to be studying stuff for university. No wonder Mrs. Stein said that it would be tough to entertain Orville.

"Well, then, it's time for fun,"

Mrs. Stein declared. "Your entertainment has arrived."

"But I want *you* to play a game with me, Mother," Orville moaned. He sounded so sad that both Tracy and Warren felt bad for him.

"Oh, I'm much too busy for games, Orville. Our book discussion group is meeting today and we're talking about the paranormal. That means ghosts," she explained to Tracy. "Such a silly idea."

Tracy and Warren could hear Johnny laughing over their heads.

"Anyway, you children have a fine time. I have to go get ready for my group."

Mrs. Stein left the kids on the porch, walking stiffly off into the house. Orville looked even sadder when she left. It was as if he'd been left behind by the one person in his life who mattered.

"C'mon, Orville," Tracy said. "Cheer

up. You're going to have a fun time with us today."

Orville just stared at Tracy as if she were out of her mind. "Fun?" he said. "I never have fun. Why would I have fun with you?"

Chapter 4

Tracy did try hard. She began with card tricks, but it seemed that Orville already knew them. Then she tried the disappearing ball trick. Except Orville saw the ball go up her sleeve. She was going to try the disappearing rabbit trick again . . . but the rabbit was too scared. He'd already taken off all by himself.

"Are those your only tricks?" Orville asked.

"No, watch this," Tracy told him. She was getting more and more desperate.

Tracy asked Warren to bring her the magic wand. Then she took a bunch of jelly beans and began stuffing them into the wand. "Presto chango!" Tracy announced. The wand was supposed to turn into a bunch of flowers.

Instead, all the jelly beans dropped onto the table.

"I hope my mom didn't pay much for this show," Orville said.

That made Tracy mad. She turned to one side and got out the *Book of Spells*. If this kid didn't like fake magic, she'd see what he thought about the real thing.

"Ich stem flavus levitas figus mod!" Tracy chanted.

"Your Latin isn't very good," Orville commented.

"It's not Latin," Tracy told him. She might have gone on to say something about the language of Fenrath, where the Book of Spells came from. But there was no time.

The Jewel of Fenrath began glowing pink, then blue. Suddenly a bolt of lightning shot out and hit two puppets lying on Orville's toy box.

The puppets got up and did a little

dance! They looked like the dancing puppets of a music box.

"How's that for magic?" Tracy asked.

"You did it with wires. That's obvious."

"Wires!" Tracy yelled. "What wires? That was magic. Real magic. I used the *Book of* . . . " Tracy didn't finish. She fig-

ured it wouldn't be smart to give every-thing away.

Instead, she went behind the shed and pulled Warren back with her.

"Hey!" Warren yelled.

"Sorry," Tracy replied. "This kid is starting to get to me. If magic isn't going to work, let's try the Monster."

"Me?"

"You see any other possible monsters around here?" Tracy replied. "Besides, if the kid isn't happy, his mom won't pay us. You want that computer game, don't you?"

"Yes," Warren said.

"And nobody else will see you. You're just part of the act – the monster part."

"Oh, okay," Warren said. "Give me the pepper."

Tracy had learned to carry pepper with her wherever she went. If they needed Warren to be the Monster, pepper made him sneeze. If they needed Warren

as a kid, pepper would change him back.
Right now, they needed the Monster.

Tracy threw some pepper in her
brother's face.

"Ah . . . ah . . . ah-choo!" Warren
replied. And then, instantly, he turned
into the Monster.

"Do you have any idea how embarrassing this is?" Warren asked. "Changing

into a large blue monster every time I sneeze."

"It's only until I figure out how to reverse the spell," Tracy told him. Then she added with a flourish, "Besides, the show must go on."

"That's right," they both heard from overhead. Suddenly Johnny the ghost became visible.

Johnny had been watching the whole thing. "Tracy, you tried hard," he said, "but that Orville is like a block of wood. Let's hope the Monster gets him going."

"Hey, Johnny," the Monster said, "can I borrow your trumpet?"

"Sure, no problem," Johnny told him. He handed the Monster his old trumpet and crossed his fingers. Johnny could only hope that Warren played better as a monster than he did as a kid.

Tracy had ducked back to the other side of the shed. Orville was sitting there holding an action toy. He looked pretty bored.

"And now," Tracy announced, "the next part of our show – the one, the only Monster!"

Chapter 5

The Monster came out playing the trumpet. He was trying to play "When the Saints Come Marching In," but a lot of the notes came out flat. Poor Johnny the ghost had to cover his ears.

"Good monster costume," Orville admitted, "but can you get this guy to stop playing? He's awful."

"Awful!" Tracy shouted. "Don't make fun of my broth . . . oops, I mean, the Monster. He's still learning. And it's not easy to play trumpet with those big blue lips."

"Obviously," Orville replied. "Mr. Monster, can you play far, far away?"

"If you hum a few bars," the Monster replied, disguising his voice.

"I don't mean the song. I mean, can

you play far, far away so I don't have to hear you."

Oh, that was mean, Tracy thought. Now she was getting *really* mad. This Orville kid was bad enough when he was just spoiled and bored. But now he was insulting her brother.

"Orville, you are nasty," Tracy told him.

"You mean 'offensive' or 'loathsome,'" Orville replied. "You really should work on your English vocabulary. It's as bad as your Latin." Orville just looked so smug.

"My vocabulary is excellent," Tracy told him. "And I know languages you haven't even heard of. Just listen to this."

Tracy grabbed the Book of Spells and began reading. *"Ich stem nimoy teherialis focarrum flek!* How do you like that?"

Orville was about to say that he wasn't impressed, but he didn't get a chance. Tracy's words had made the jewel begin to glow. It glowed green, then blue, then greener, then bluer . . . and finally the lightning shot out.

"Duck!" yelled the Monster.

Tracy, Orville and the Monster all hit the ground. The blue lightning bolt zoomed around, looking for someplace to strike. Finally, it found a target – Orville's plastic action figure!

Orville's action figure was not usually

a scary thing. It was small, red and robot-like. It could bend in lots of directions, but didn't do many tricks. But that was before the magic lightning struck!

Suddenly, the action figure was even bigger than the Monster!

"Tracy," the Monster said, terrified, "what have you done?"

"It looks like I made a little mistake," Tracy admitted.

"But that was a really good trick," Orville told her. "I think I'm starting to like your show."

Tracy smiled, but not for long. Over by the garden bench, Orville's very large action figure was starting to move. Bolts of electricity flashed across its helmet. From deep down, all the children could hear its voice.

"I am King . . . King of the Universe!"

Chapter 6

The giant action figure was truly impressive. The King of the Universe stood up, sparks flying, its mighty arms stretched out. Tracy and the Monster crouched in fear, but Orville thought this was great.

"Now that's a good trick," Orville commented. "Maybe you can explain to me the science behind all that. Do you use a molecule generator? Do you change the atomic structure?"

"I . . . uh . . . " Tracy, for once, was speechless.

"Oh, never mind. I just want to go for a ride," Orville declared. With that, he went off and climbed up the back of his giant action figure. Soon he was perched on top of its head. Orville and the King of the Universe raced back and forth in the garden. Orville was laughing like crazy.

"Looks like the kid is having the time of his life," commented Johnny the ghost. He had popped up over their heads.

Tracy sighed. "I guess he'll write us a good review in the morning paper. But somehow I've got to get the toy

back to normal size." She picked up the Book of Spells. "Let me just check the index . . . "

"Tracy," the Monster said, "please get it right this time."

Tracy just shook her head. She couldn't understand why the Monster should be so scared. After all, he was almost as big as the King of the Universe. In a second, Tracy thought, she'd get it all straightened out.

But before Tracy could find the words to reverse her spell, Mrs. Stein came out of the house. Quickly, Tracy stuck the jewel beneath the patio bench.

"Oh, children," she said, "I see the Monster has arrived."

"Uh, yes," the Monster said in a disguised voice, "here I am. That was me playing the trumpet."

"Yes," Mrs. Stein said, clearing her throat. "You were, uh, trying very hard. Do you know the Haydn trumpet concerto?"

The Monster just smiled. "No, I'm still trying to learn 'Far, Far Away.'"

"Yes, indeed," replied Mrs. Stein. "And where might Orville be?"

"Orville? Orville?" Tracy replied. She was glad that Mrs. Stein hadn't seen her son riding on the King of the Universe. But she wasn't exactly sure where Orville had gone. "Uh, he went out to play with his action toy because, uh, because . . . "

"Because it's intermission," the Monster said brightly.

Tracy shot her brother a look of relief. "Yes, it's intermission. It's in the contract, Mrs. Stein – rules of the Monster and Magic Union."

Mrs. Stein just laughed. "Well, I'm so glad he's having a good time with your show. Now I'll let you get ready . . . oh, what's this?"

Mrs. Stein saw the Jewel of Fenrath beneath the patio bench. She bent down to pick it up, holding the jewel in her hand. "Hmm. A jewel. Must have fallen off the chandelier in the living room. Most unusual."

With that, Mrs. Stein slipped the Jewel of Fenrath into her pocket.

"Mrs. Stein, wait . . . " Tracy begged.

But the kitchen phone began ringing before Tracy could finish. Mrs. Stein said a quick "excuse me" and then took off into the house.

That left Tracy and the Monster to stare at each other.

"How are you going to reverse the spell without the jewel?" the Monster asked.

"I can't," Tracy wailed. "My magic show flopped. The monster show didn't really work. Orville's gone off with a giant action toy. And now Mrs. Stein has the jewel. This is as bad as it gets."

Tracy was absolutely right in what she said – except for the last item. Things were bad, all right, but they were about to get worse.

The King of the Universe came around the porch and right up to the

Monster. He looked at the Monster with
a dull robot stare.

    "You are an intruder! Surrender or be
destroyed!"

Chapter 7

"Oh, sorry," the Monster told the giant action figure. "I didn't mean to intrude."

The King of the Universe was not impressed by the Monster's polite answer. He merely repeated himself. "You are an intruder. Surrender or be destroyed."

The Monster decided that the King of the Universe wasn't very bright. He thought it would be best to play along. "Okay, I surrender. Are you happy now?"

"I am the King of the Universe," the action figure said. Little Orville was standing beside him, enjoying all this.

"Okay, no problem," the Monster agreed. "You can be King of whatever."

"No, he can't!" Tracy told him. She was known to shoot off her mouth at the most awkward times, and this was one of them. "That guy is just an oversized hunk of plastic. He's just a big bully with an attitude!"

The King of the Universe may not have been very bright, but he did know when he was being insulted.

"Who is this underling?" he asked.

"Underling? I'm no underling!" Tracy told him. "I'll have you know that I'm in charge of the Monster and Magic Show."

The King of the Universe was not impressed. "You will be destroyed!"

Luckily, the King of the Universe did not have any real weapons close at hand. All he had was a beach pail full of plastic balls. He quickly pulled one out and threw it right at the Monster.

"Ow!" the Monster cried. "That hurt!"

Little Orville was watching all this and laughing like crazy. He thought it was all part of the show. For him, it was like Saturday morning cartoons in real life!

"Ow, ow!" cried the Monster when two more plastic balls connected with his head.

"C'mon, Monster, fight back!" Tracy urged.

The Monster didn't have much choice. When the King of the Universe threw a fourth ball, the Monster caught it. Then, using his monster strength, he threw it right back at the giant action figure.

Boiiing! The ball connected. The King of the Universe staggered backwards, holding his head.

"Oh, I'm sorry," the Monster apologized. "Sometimes I don't know my own strength."

Tracy shook her head. "You don't have to apologize. He was trying to hurt you. You were just defending yourself."

The Monster tried to explain. "But now he's mad, Tracy. He could be dangerous!"

The King of the Universe really was dangerous. He had great strength and an electric zapper on his head. He might have used those against Tracy and the Monster, but he didn't have a chance.

At that moment, all three of them were being attacked by a toy plane!

Zzzzzzooooom!

Orville had decided to join the fun. He was at the controls of his toy plane, dive-bombing them all.

"This is so much fun!" Orville laughed.

The King of the Universe was not

pleased. He'd been whacked by a plastic ball. Now he was being buzzed by a toy plane. He was mad!

The giant action figure turned towards Orville. "*You* are the intruder! You must be destroyed!"

Chapter 8

Mrs. Stein knew nothing about what was happening in her backyard. She had no idea that the Monster was real and not a man in a costume. She didn't know that the Jewel of Fenrath on her kitchen table was the key to Tracy's magic. And she couldn't see that a giant action figure was about to attack her son.

Mrs. Stein was too busy to notice. She was yapping on the phone to a member of her book club.

"Ghosts, dear? You must be joking. There is just no proof of any paranormal experience," she said. "Par-a-normal, just as I said," Mrs. Stein went on. "It means things that are beyond the normal world, of course. And there just aren't any such things."

Johnny the ghost was trying to get the Jewel of Fenrath back to Tracy. From the look of things outside, he had better hurry.

Still, he was interested in this conversation. He made himself invisible and listened in.

"Oh, that's so silly," Mrs. Stein went on. "Ghosts are only products of people's

imagination. No, I'm not calling your Aunt Sadie a nitwit, but there are no ghosts. None. They're impossible."

Mrs. Stein sounded so sure of herself. Maybe that's why Johnny decided to have some fun. He went over to the radio and changed it from classical to dance music.

"Hmm," said Mrs. Stein. "Early in the day for a rumba." Still, Mrs. Stein rather liked this old-fashioned dance. She began to hum along.

Johnny picked up a basting brush and tickled her.

"Hee-hee-hee. Ooh, that tickles!"

Mrs. Stein looked around and realized that she was all alone. There was nobody around to tickle her. And THAT, she thought, was very strange.

But not as strange as when she turned back to the counter. There was an egg in mid-air!

"Oh my," she said, reaching out to

catch the egg. The egg, of course, was not falling. It was in Johnny's invisible hand.

As soon as Mrs. Stein had the egg, Johnny lifted the butter and the flour. Now THEY seemed to be floating in mid-air!

"Oh, oh, oh my goodness!" exclaimed Mrs. Stein.

Johnny began to toss the butter and flour to Mrs. Stein. Soon the two of them were juggling all three items. Butter, egg and flour were sailing back and forth between them.

Until Johnny missed a catch.

"Oops," Johnny said, as all three went falling to the floor.

Mrs. Stein did not hear the "oops," but she did see the mess on the floor. She also saw a mop come in her direction. The mop seemed to be dancing – and it had a pot on top of its handle. It looked an awful lot like a ballroom dancer in a 1940s movie!

"What on earth?" asked Mrs. Stein as the mop bowed and tipped its pot in her direction. "You want to dance?"

The mop, of course, couldn't answer. But the pot up at its top nodded yes. Soon Mrs. Stein was dancing the rumba with a very talented mop!

"Oh, you're such a wonderful dancer!" she cooed to the mop.

Johnny might have said that Mrs. Stein was quite a good dancer herself, but decided not to. Actually, he was enjoying himself. He hadn't done the rumba since 1942, back during the war. Ah, he thought, people could dance back then.

But Johnny couldn't let his memories interfere with the job at hand. He had to get the jewel back to Tracy!

When the music stopped, Mrs. Stein realized that she was dancing with a mop with a pail on its handle. This was truly embarrassing. The only way to explain it was, well, a ghost. And Mrs. Stein was sure there was no such thing as ghosts.

This was strange, very strange, she thought. But it had been fun.

"One more number?" Mrs. Stein asked – speaking to no one at all. "I'd love to do the cha-cha!"

Johnny would have enjoyed the

chance to cha-cha as well. It was a great Latin dance 60 years ago, and Johnny still knew the steps. But outside he heard a clanking sound. He looked out the window to see the King of the Universe about to attack Orville!

"Maybe later," he said to the amazed Mrs. Stein. Then he grabbed the jewel from her pocket and flew outside to help the kids.

Chapter 9

The King of the Universe was about to strike Orville when Tracy stepped between them.

"Pick on somebody your own size," she said.

Tracy was quite fearless . . . and sometimes quite foolish. She was not at all the size of the King of the Universe. In fact, Tracy was about one-third his size. Still, she stood her ground until the giant action figure picked her up.

"The underling must be destroyed," said the King of the Universe.

"Put me down!" Tracy demanded.

The King did not put her down — in fact, he hung her up! There was a clothesline just over their heads. In a second, Tracy was pinned up on the line.

"Help me!" Tracy cried.

When the Monster saw his sister in big trouble, he knew he had to do something.

"Leave her alone!" the Monster yelled. He tried to sound as fierce as he could, but it was hard. The Monster still

had Warren's squeaky eight-year-old voice.

Quickly, the Monster pulled at the clothesline. In a few seconds, he had yanked Tracy down to his end of the yard. Then he took off the clothespins and Tracy fell to the ground with a thud.

"Sorry," the Monster said.

"It's the thought that counts," Tracy told him.

Over at the side of the yard, the King of the Universe had cornered Orville.

"You cannot escape my wrath!" said the giant action figure.

"Oh, this is such a good show," replied Orville. He tried to seem fearless, but now he was really scared. After all, a very large action figure was towering over him.

Tracy and the Monster knew that this

wasn't part of the show. Orville was in real danger.

"Don't move!" Tracy called. "I'll save you!"

The Monster gave Tracy a look. The look said, how? The King of the Universe was three times bigger and 20 times stronger than Tracy. What could she do?

"I mean, the Monster will save you!"

Oh great, the Monster thought. Still, he didn't have much choice. He worked up all the courage he had and jumped at the King of the Universe.

The battle between the two of them wasn't all that exciting. The King of the Universe was pretty clumsy. The Monster didn't know how to box or wrestle. The result was a lot of grunting and groaning, but not much action.

"C'mon, you guys. This is a fake fight. Do something!" yelled Orville.

The Monster knew it was quite a real fight, but wasn't sure what to do next. On TV, the good guys always have some wrestling move that saves the day. The Monster tried. He grabbed the King of the Universe in an arm hold. The giant action toy twisted free. Then he tried a leg hold that should have thrown his opponent to the ground. Instead, the Monster got a kick in his jaw.

"Ouch!" he cried.

Wrestling moves just weren't working. The Monster decided to give the King of the Universe a big push with his shoulder. That worked. The giant action toy fell backwards onto a pile of fertilizer.

"Way to go!" Tracy shouted.

For a second, the Monster was very pleased with himself. The King of the Universe was flat on his back. He wasn't moving any more. The only problem was a cloud of fertilizer dust.

I wonder if I'm allergic to fertilizer dust? the Monster thought.

His nose answered the question. "Ah . . . ah . . . ah-choo!"

Suddenly the Monster disappeared. In his place was eight-year-old Warren Patterson. Warren was only slightly bigger than Orville. Tracy was only slightly bigger than Warren. Even the three of them together were no match for the King of the Universe.

But the King of the Universe was nowhere in sight!

Chapter 10

"Where'd he go?" Warren asked.

"Where'd they both go?" wondered Orville. Both the Monster and the King of the Universe had suddenly disappeared.

"Well, the Monster, uh, he had to put some money in a parking meter . . . " Warren told the boy. "And the action figure guy, well, uh . . . "

Warren didn't have time to finish. With an incredible roar, the King of the Universe came out of the garden shed. He was riding on a lawn tractor – and he was coming right at them.

"Run!" yelled Tracy.

"Good idea," agreed her brother.

Soon all three of the children were

running across the backyard. They were being chased by a giant action figure on a lawn tractor!

Orville jumped up on a lawn chair that collapsed under his weight. The chair seemed to swallow him up!

"Oh, my gosh!" Tracy cried.

"We've got to get him out!" Warren agreed.

The two kids struggled to open the

lawn chair. As they worked, the King of the Universe just laughed. He sat on the lawn tractor and got ready to mow the three of them down. Just as they pulled Orville free, the King gunned the lawn tractor's motor. He was coming at them.

"Is this part of the show?" asked Orville.

"I wish it were," Warren replied.

"What we need is that monster back," Orville suggested. "He'd save the day!"

Much as Warren appreciated the boy's confidence, there wasn't much he could do except . . . sneeze. How could he make himself sneeze before the King of the Universe mowed them down?

What was that? Down on the lawn was one dandelion – one old fluffy dandelion. All Warren had to do was hide behind the shed, take a sniff, and his allergy would do the rest.

"Ah . . . ah . . . ah-choo!"

Warren became the Monster. He raced back to where Tracy and Orville were cowering beneath the lawn chair.

Just as the King of the Universe gunned the mower, the Monster was back. With hardly any effort, he reached out and stopped the lawn tractor with his bare hands.

"Way to go, Monster!" shouted Orville.

The Monster was basking in this approval when Johnny the ghost finally flew out to them. He had the Jewel of Fenrath in his hand.

"Johnny, what took you so long?" Tracy asked.

"I wanted to finish that rumba," the ghost told her. "But here, go ahead with the reversing spell."

Tracy began to chant. *"Ich stem fluvayus levitas figus mod. Brickenblaxen!"*

The jewel began glowing again. Then a bolt of blue-green lightning shot out of the jewel. It sailed around the yard until it found the action figure.

KAZZZOOOOP!

Suddenly the King of the Universe was just a tiny hunk of plastic on the lawn.

"Wow!" said Orville. "That was awesome."

"Thanks," Tracy replied. "A little practice and it's easy." She slipped the jewel into her pocket to keep it safe.

"Here comes my mother," Orville said. "And there's a funny look on her face."

Chapter 11

Orville had no reason to be worried about the look on his mother's face. She wasn't angry. She wasn't upset that he wasn't working on flash cards or math problems.

The look on her face was very simple – Mrs. Stein was happy.

"Mother, are you okay?" Orville asked.

"Oh, yes, yes, quite divine, really!" replied his mother. "I've just had the most extraordinary experience. I was dancing . . . "

"Dancing?" Orville asked. "By yourself?"

"Not exactly by myself," Mrs. Stein tried to explain. "It was as if someone else was there. And it was all quite fabulous in the most extraordinary way."

Orville looked at his mother as if she had lost her mind. Up above, Johnny the ghost winked at Tracy and the Monster.

"You know, Orville," his mother went on, "I think we've been far too serious around here. We need to have some more fun, don't you think? A chance to spend some time together and just, well, just have fun."

"No flash cards?"

"No flash cards," replied his mother.

"No philosophy problems?"

"No problems of any kind," said Mrs. Stein. "Just fun, like today. You did have a good time today, didn't you?"

"It was awesome, Mom! My action figure came alive, and Tracy got hung on a clothesline, and the Monster had to save me . . ."

"Orville, you are getting quite an imagination. I guess that's what happens when you start having a good time."

Mrs. Stein turned to Tracy and the Monster. "You two have done a wonderful job. Here's the fee for your show – and a little bonus because it worked out so well."

"Thanks, Mrs. Stein," Tracy said.

"Thank you, dear. I don't think Orville will ever be the same after all the fun today. In fact, I don't think I'll be the same, either. Mr. Monster, do you know how to cha-cha?"

"Sorry, I've got two left feet," the Monster told her in a deep voice.

Then Tracy had an idea. "But we know a guy named Johnny who likes to dance. I'll have him give you a call."

End

TOP SECRET!

Sneak Preview of New Monster By Mistake Episodes

Even more all-new monster-iffic episodes of Monster by Mistake are on the way in 2003 and 2004! Here's an inside look at what's ahead for Warren, Tracy and Johnny:

- It promises to be a battle royale when a superstar wrestler comes to town and challenges the Monster to a match at the Pickford arena.
- There's a gorilla on the loose in Pickford, but where did it come from? It's up to the Monster, Tracy and Johnny to catch it and solve the mystery.
- When making deliveries for a bakery, Warren discovers who robbed the Pickford Savings and Loan. Can the Monster stop the robbers from getting away?
- Warren, Tracy and Johnny visit Fenrath, the home to Gorgool, the Book of Spells and the jewel. In Fenrath, they discover who imprisoned Gorgool in the ball and what they must do in order to restore order to this magical kingdom.

MONSTER By Mistake!   Videos

Six Monster by Mistake home videos are
available and more are on the way.

Each video contains 2 episodes and comes with a special Monster surprise!

Only $9.99 each.

Monster by Mistake & Entertaining Orville
1-55366-130-3

Fossel Remains & Kidnapped 1-55366-131-1

Monster a Go-Go & Home Alone 1-55366-132-X

Billy Caves In & Tracy's Jacket 1-55366-202-4

Campsite Creeper & Johnny's Reunion
1-55366-201-6

Gorgools' Pet & Jungle Land
1-55366-200-8

About the people who brought you this book

Located in Toronto, Canada, **Cambium** has been producing quality family entertainment since 1982. Some of their best known shows are *Sharon Lois and Bram's The Elephant Show, Eric's World*, and of course, *Monster By Mistake*!

Catapult Productions in Toronto wants to entertain the whole world with computer animation. Now that we've entertained you, there are only 5 billion people to go!

Mark Mayerson grew up loving animated cartoons and now has a job making them. *Monster By Mistake* is the first TV show he created.

Paul Kropp is an author, editor and educator. His work includes young adult novels, novels for reluctant readers, and the bestselling *How to Make Your Child a Reader for Life*.